For Peter
and Lisa
M. W.

For Lewis
and Thomas
B. F.

First U.S. edition 2005

Library of Congress Cataloging-in-Publication Data is available.

Library of Congress Catalog Card Number 2004057472

ISBN 0-7636-2439-X

2 4 6 8 10 9 7 5 3 1

Printed in China

This book was typeset in Columbus MT.
The illustrations were done in watercolor, ink, and pencil.

Candlewick Press
2067 Massachusetts Avenue
Cambridge, Massachusetts 02140

visit us at www.candlewick.com

Sleep Tight, Little Bear

Martin Waddell

illustrated by Barbara Firth

CANDLEWICK PRESS
CAMBRIDGE, MASSACHUSETTS

Once there were two bears,

Big Bear and Little Bear.

Big Bear is the big bear,

and Little Bear is the little bear.

One day, while Big Bear was busy,

Little Bear went out to play.

Little Bear climbed up the rocks

above the Bear Cave. There was a place

there, little-bear-size or just a bit bigger.

"I could have my own bear cave in here!"

thought Little Bear. "With a bed

and a table and a chair."

"Little Bear!" called Big Bear,

looking out of the Bear Cave.

"Little Bear! Little Bear!"

called Big Bear, coming out of the cave.

"LITTLE BEAR!"

called Big Bear, but he couldn't

see Little Bear anywhere.

"I'm up here, Big Bear!"

called Little Bear.

"I've made my own cave!"

Big Bear climbed up the rocks

above the Bear Cave,

and Little Bear showed

Big Bear his cave.

"That's my bear chair and my table,

and this is my bed," Little Bear said.

"It's a good cave," said Big Bear.

"I need lots more things,"

Little Bear said.

Big Bear helped Little Bear

carry things up the rocks to the cave.

Little Bear played

all day in his cave.

Little Bear swept

his cave.

Little Bear read

his book.

Little Bear made

his bed.

Little Bear jumped

on his bed.

"Suppertime, Little Bear!"

called Big Bear.

"Could I have my supper up here?" Little Bear asked.

"Well . . ." said Big Bear.

"*Please*, Big Bear?" Little Bear said.

"Well . . . all right, Little Bear,"

said Big Bear.

And Little Bear had his supper

in his own little cave.

Then it was bedtime.

"Can I sleep up here?" Little Bear asked.

"All right, Little Bear," said Big Bear,

and he tucked Little Bear up into bed.

"Sleep tight, Little Bear," said Big Bear.

"I'll be in the Bear Cave if you need me."

Big Bear plodded all the way back

to the Bear Cave alone,

without Little Bear.

Little Bear sat up in bed and looked around.

"I'm a big bear in a cave of my own,"

Little Bear told himself.

Little Bear looked out of his cave at the moon

shining through the dark trees.

"Big Bear might be lonely without me,"

thought Little Bear.

Little Bear climbed out of bed.

"I wonder if Big Bear's missing me,"

Little Bear said to himself.

And he went to see Big Bear.

"You forgot to read me

my story, Big Bear," Little Bear said,

climbing up on the Bear Chair.

"I'll read to you now," said Big Bear.

"Did you miss me, Big Bear?" asked Little Bear.

"I missed you a lot, Little Bear," said Big Bear.

"I could stay here tonight so that you

won't be lonely, Big Bear,"

Little Bear said.

"I'd like that a lot, Little Bear,"

said Big Bear.

And Big Bear read Little Bear

the Bear Book by the light of the fire.

Big Bear sat in the Bear Chair

with his arms close around Little Bear

till the logs on the fire had burned low.

"Sleep tight, Little Bear,"

whispered Big Bear.

But Little Bear

was already . . .

asleep.